A Treasure's Trove

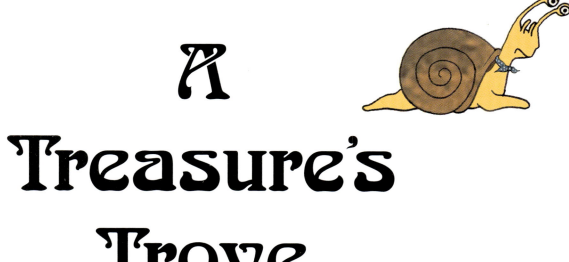

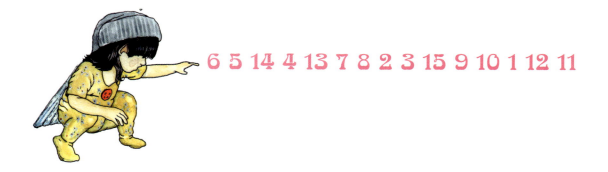

A Treasure's Trove

A Fairy Tale about Real Treasure for Parents and Children of All Ages

Written and Illustrated
by Michael Stadther

Treasure Trove, Inc.

Production
Color Group

Artist Assistant
Alex Reiter

to Helen

Published in the United States by Treasure Trove, Inc.
Printed in Mexico

Visit www.atreasurestrove.com
for information on the treasure hunt.

ISBN 0-9760618-2-1

First Edition
Second Printing

Contents

Prologue 14
The Beginning

Chapter one 16
Zac and Pook

Chapter two 20
The Great Forest

Chapter three 22
Dragonfly and Spider

Chapter four 25
The Forest Creatures

Chapter five 28
Talking Trees

Chapter six 32
The Ladybug's Plan

Chapter seven 35
Ana

Chapter eight 45
Yorah

Chapter nine 48
The Jewelry Box

Chapter ten 52
Yorah Understands

Chapter eleven 55
Rusful

Chapter tweleve 59
Yorah's Plan

Chapter thirteen 63
The Theft

Chapter fourteen 66
Rusful's Return

Chapter fifteen 69
The Anniversary

Chapter sixteen 73
The Jewels are Hidden in the Forest

Chapter seventeen 78
The Hostage

Chapter eighteen 88
The Ransom

Chapter nineteen 94
The Rain

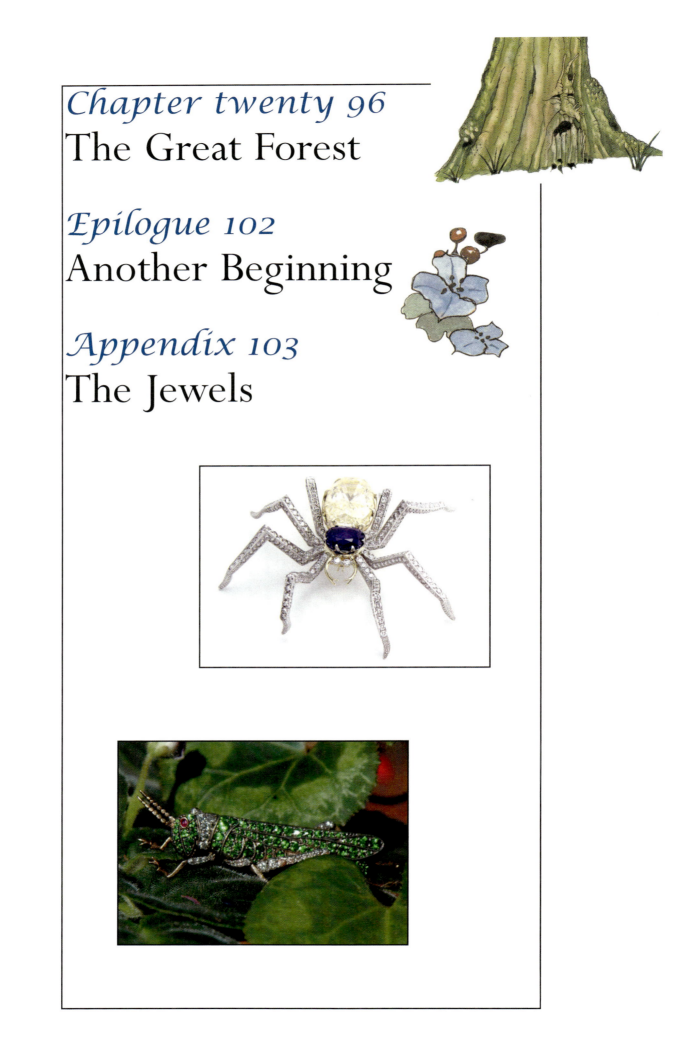

Chapter twenty 96
The Great Forest

Epilogue 102
Another Beginning

Appendix 103
The Jewels

Foreword

This Fairy Tale takes place in a Great Forest and tells a sweet (and sometimes sad) story about friendship and greed, Good Fairies and Evil Fairies and how love is greater than fear.

Also, concealed in the pages of this story, are the clues to twelve very real and very valuable treasures that I have hidden around the continental United States for you to find and keep—treasures similar to the jeweled Forest Creatures in the Fairy Tale. I have selected these treasures from all around the world, and I think that they are all beautiful.

I have not hidden them in remote locations, but rather I have hidden them in places accessible to everyone. You might even find one by accident, as you walk across a field or down a street. But none are on private property and none are buried. Nothing needs to be lifted or moved for you to find them. But I have hidden them well.

The simple clues don't need any special knowledge to find or decipher. Anyone who can read can discover the exact location of each treasure—just the way one of the characters does in the story.

I hope you find them. But I also hope that this book is more than a treasure hunt. I hope that you enjoy reading it, and that you take time to read it to a child. I hope it reminds you and the child that we have to take care of each other, and take care of the earth. Oh, yes—and not to be afraid of the dark.

So, as you read and look carefully at the illustrations, if you believe in Fairies, you may find the clues that will lead you to the treasures.

Michael Stadther

P.S. I have tried to make all the puzzles in this book solvable—but if I have failed in my task, then the treasures will become mine again, and their hiding places will be revealed on December 31, 2007.

Finally, there are two ways to solve the puzzle…

1) You can decipher the clues in the book, go to the precise location of the treasure and claim your treasure, or

2) You can find the twelve jeweled creatures and their mates hidden within the pages of this book and, while you cannot claim the real treasures if you find them here, I hope you will share the experience of looking for them with a child.

And this will be your treasure.

13

Prologue: The Beginning

Not Long Ago …

Snail knew that she had ventured too far from the linden stump. She knew that it would be night soon and the dark dust would begin to fall. Her husband, also known as Snail, had warned her to be under the linden stump by dusk to avoid the dust that fell every night, crystallizing the Forest. But now the distant birch grove was cast in grays and purples and she could see the dark clouds forming on the horizon. She didn't think that she would make it.

Gradually, she crawled toward the birch grove and the linden stump—the last green area in this part of the Forest. She could see Spider and Beetle in the hole under the distant linden stump and she knew they would protect the other Creatures within. Caterpillar, Ant and Grasshopper would be huddled together and her husband, Snail, would be anxiously awaiting her arrival. Dragonfly, Hummingbird, Butterfly, Firefly, Bee and Ladybug would soon be flying in.

All of the other creatures had lost their mates to the dark dust. One by one they had been caught at night, touched by the dark dust and crystallized. And then, mysteriously, they vanished.

She and Snail were the last of the couples. Ironically, the slowest of the twelve couples had survived the longest.

She could now see the dark boiling clouds forming overhead. The wisps of clouds dipped toward the ground like hands grabbing at the Forest floor. Then she could see the dark dust sifting down through the trees. Softly, gently drifting toward the Forest floor, crystallizing the leaves and the plants that it fell upon.

Snail, once moving so slowly that it was hardly noticeable, now moved not at all—frozen in place. Snail had become a beautiful crystallized jewel.

Above her motionless body, the clouds dipped even lower—although they were not clouds at all but rather a boiling mass of dark bodies with leathery wings and grasping claws seeking their desired treasure.

Then, a yellow ulcerous hand reached down from the dark mass, and plucked Snail from the ground. Then, as rapidly as the dark mass appeared, it moved on and Snail was gone…

Chapter 1

Zac and Pook

acharevah and Pook had walked slowly through the Great Forest for most of the day, but now, as they climbed a small ridge toward the birch grove, Zac wanted to move faster—the sun would be setting soon, and Pook was afraid of the dark. But he couldn't hurry a timid doth like Pook, especially uphill; so they climbed together, at Pook's pokey pace.

Woodcarvers like Zac often kept doths for protection. Usually, doths barked bravely to warn their masters about lurking tam-o'jacks and tool-stealing grubinmoles and they flew rapidly on their powerful moth-like wings. Their tenacity and strong jaws could even fend off a prowling cawcat. But not Pook.

Pook wasn't like most doths—he was clumsy, fat and he was afraid of almost everything—especially the dark. Yet, it didn't matter to Zac because he had raised his best friend from a chrysalis.

Once they reached the grove, Zac hoped to find a fallen silver birch limb—the final piece he needed to finish the jewelry box. He had worked on the box for almost a year, and it would be the most beautiful one that he had ever made—more beautiful than any of the boxes or wooden toys and puzzles that he sold in the village. Zac would complete the box tonight, so that he could give it to Ana tomorrow—their first wedding anniversary.

As they neared the top of the ridge, Zac became a little weary of Pook's dawdling. "Let's get a move on," he said. He stooped, scooped his hands around the fat doth's sides, and tossed him up the ridge. Midair, Pook beat his wings frantically and spread his short legs, preparing for what he knew would be a hard, two-or-three-bounce landing.

Zac loved Pook's big broad head, his constant smile and his silly "uff uff" bark that sounded more like a puff than a bark. In fact, it seemed as if Pook were afraid to bark out loud. But most of all, Zac loved the

17

sight of his doth grunting and bouncing, flapping his undersized wings, his four feet and tail spreading in all directions. It always made him laugh out loud.
Zac might as well have thrown a tigerwood stick for him to fetch. No sooner had Pook bounced and skidded to a stop than he turned and ran back down the slope, grunted and launched himself into the air, confident that Zac would catch him.

"What a good, fat doth," Zac managed to wheeze. His best friend had knocked the wind out of him. Pook wiggled in Zac's arms, licked him fully in the face, leaned his head back and smiled broadly.

Pook wiggled in Zac's arms, licked him fully
in the face, leaned his head back and smiled broadly

Chapter 2

The Great Forest

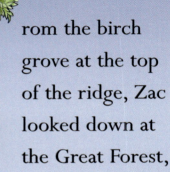

rom the birch grove at the top of the ridge, Zac looked down at the Great Forest, through which he and Pook had walked.

As far as the horizon, most of the trees gleamed black. To Zac, it looked as if a giant hand had spilled an inkwell over them. Zac knew that the Great Forest was dying, and he believed that the dust—the dark dust that fell every night, caused the blight. First, black boiling clouds filled the sky, groaning and swelling, blocking out the moon and stars. But no rain ever fell from those dark clouds—it hadn't rained in the dying Forest for almost a year.

Softly, the dark dust sifted down, whispering through the tree tops, drifting to the forest floor, smothering every green thing, every weed and flower. By morning, everything it touched hardened like cold, black glass.

So far, the blight had spared this hilltop grove of several dozen elegant birches and tall pines. After breathing the ashy atmosphere of the dying forest, Zac thought the sweet air seemed as if it smelled green. He felt a sudden cool breeze, with a threat of nightfall in it touch his cheek. The pine needles rustled, the birch leaves shivered, and Pook gave a nervous sigh. Zac began pacing, head down, scouring the ground for the wood he needed, a fallen birch limb.

Then, for a moment, he stopped and listened. Somewhere above, he could have sworn he heard the buzz of a dragonfly. But no dragonflies had flown in his part of the forest for a long time.

Chapter 3
Dragonfly and Spider

ragonfly dart-
ed in and out
among the
treetops,
observing Zac
and Pook. He
observed everything—he was the Air
Group leader in this part of
the Forest. He flew several
high-altitude
reconnaissance

passes, just to be sure, and confirmed the sighting to himself. "A human. Another human has come to destroy the Forest."

He knew his duty. He instantly banked in a tight curve and flew swiftly to inform Spider, the Ground Leader. She would devise a cunning plan to eliminate this human intruder.

Zac caught a twinkling glimpse of the dragonfly, beyond the edge of the grove, a sparkling fleck in the air. "Nice blue dragonfly," he thought.

Spider, tucked behind the hem of the web she had woven across the mouth of the knothole in the ginkgo tree, waited.

Dragonfly hovered. "Spider!"

Spider, silent and motionless, preferred to think things through and wait for the right moment. When she attacked, she killed. Of course, she only killed to eat, but she wouldn't tell that to Dragonfly. She enjoyed her menacing reputation.

"I know you can see me, Spider. Come out. I saw a human in the birch grove!"

Spider scrambled so rapidly to the center of her web that she seemed to appear there by magic. The web hardly moved.

Dragonfly awaited his orders. He deeply respected Spider, but never turned his back on her. He never trusted anyone he couldn't look in the eye, and never knew which of the Spider's eight eyes to look into.

"Tie him up," said Spider. She paused and rolled her two largest eyes skyward as if she were thinking. "Hang him up," she said, and paused again, as if formulating a deviously complex strategy. "Eat him up," she concluded.

"Begging your pardon, but permit me to inform you that the human in the birch grove is very much bigger than we are. In my opinion, unilateral aggressive action would almost certainly get us killed."

Spider paid no attention to Dragonfly's objections. She refined her instructions. "Analyze, attack, then devour."

"I suggest," persisted Dragonfly, "a combined attack. You muster the Ground Forces; I'll gather the Air Force. We'll rendezvous at base camp at the linden stump. That is all." Dragonfly buzzed away.

"I would prefer to eat the human with some dandelion greens and a nice honeysuckle wine," thought Spider.

Chapter 4
The Forest Creatures

Because Spider's entire army lived under the flat limestone rock near the linden stump, they didn't take long to assemble. Spider organized them with great precision: Snail rode atop Grasshopper to provide low level advance reconnaissance, Beetle and Ant covered the flanks, and slow Caterpillar served as rear guard. When they arrived at the stump, Dragonfly, already there, hovered impatiently and behind him hovered Bee,

Butterfly, Ladybug, Firefly and Hummingbird. Dragonfly settled on the stump and peered over a brickcap mushroom. For a moment he surveyed the troops in silence, as if to emphasize the gravity of the situation. Then, he began his oration.

"My fellow Forest Creatures. Sadly, I must report that yet another human is among us and I know that this new human is as evil as the Blight-Spreader human who the Darklings carry aloft at night and who scatters the dark dust.

"Since the beginning of time, we have shared the Forest with the Darklings. We know these vile, destructive, shadow lurking dark fairies spoil food, spread plague and carry infection. But now they have a leader, the human who spreads the blight . . ."

Like many fearless leaders, Dragonfly liked to make long speeches, in which he told his audience in great detail things they already knew. But they enjoyed it.

Firefly became so agitated that his taillight began to flash uncontrollably.

They booed and hissed at the mention of their enemies, the Darklings and the Blight-Spreader. They shuddered and murmured in fear when he described the nightly falling of the dark dust. They wept when he recalled their missing loved ones. Each of them mourned a relative or mate who had been touched by the dust and transformed into a shining stone—another jewel for the Blight-Spreader's collection.

"But now," said Dragonfly, repeating his concern, "another human walks among us and we must stop him."

He dismissed the Butterfly's proposal to send a delegation to ask the human, nicely of course, to please leave. He convinced the furious Spider and Bee not to fly off immediately and attack. And in the end, everyone listened attentively as Dragonfly outlined his strategy.

"First," he said, "I will lead the Air Corps, in flight formation delta. We will conduct aerial surveillance of the human. Simultaneously, Spider and the Ground Forces will move in for close, direct observation. We will then rendezvous back here at base camp and prepare our final assault."

"Then we eat him," thought Spider.

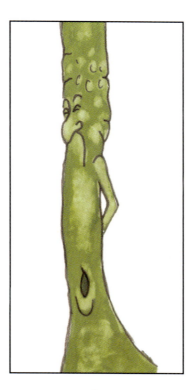

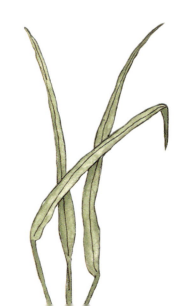

Chapter 5

Talking Trees

hile the Forest Creatures met, Zac searched the birch grove for the wood he needed, Pook helpfully wrestled the small hand ax from Zac's tool bag and, with the handle in his jaws, held the blade against the base of one of the largest birch trees. To get Zac's attention, he managed a small "uff."

"Thanks, Pook. Good boy. But we're not cutting down any of these trees. These trees are alive." He thought that Ana would be proud of him for saying that.

Alive? Pook cocked his head, puzzled. Zac bent down and whispered, trying to sound mysterious, "They can even talk to you, Pook."

Pook's droopy-topped ears shot up.

"Listen to them," Zac whispered, trying not to laugh.

Pook dropped the ax, lowered his rear end, backed up a couple of steps and tried pulling his head into his body like a turtle. He looked around nervously. Talking trees—something else to worry about.

28

How bad could it get?

"So, to finish the jewelry box for Ana, we have to find a fallen tree, or a branch broken from the trunk," said Zac, intending to resume his search of the grove.

Pook, however, backed himself up on top of Zac's boot, with every intention of staying there. Zac didn't care that a frightened doth was riding his right boot. Pook was his best friend.

Dragging Pook, he limped across the grove and leaned over a large, moss-covered limestone rock beside the tallest of the birches. There he saw what he had hoped to see—a freshly fallen limb, just the right size. He gently shook Pook off his boot and picked up the branch, completely unaware of Dragonfly's Air Corps high overhead, or Spider's Ground Forces approaching among the roots.

Zac sat on the rock and, with his hatchet, first cleaned the limb of smaller branches, then trimmed it to a size he could carry back down the ridge. When he had finished, he stood on top of the rock and, with his curved pruning saw, carefully smoothed the jagged place where the dead limb had broken away from the living tree. "Sorry," he whispered. "This will only hurt for a second." He brushed the new cut clean, and smeared it with soothing beeswax.

While Zac concentrated on doctoring the birch tree, Pook dramatically struck his bravest guard-doth pose and softly 'uffed' at the spider and other tiny creatures who were observing Zac from behind a fallen pinecone.

"There," said Zac, admiring his handiwork. "That's how we have to take care of the trees, Pook. Now, we'd better get going if we want to be home before dark."

Dark? The word rang in Pook's ears, terrifying him. Things had gone from bad to worse. He turned his attention away from Spider's army and considered the likelihood that talking trees in the dark would soon surround him!

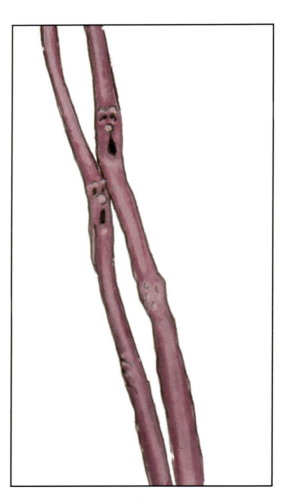

He had turned his attention away
from Spider's army and considered
the likelihood that talking trees
in the dark would soon
surround him!

Chapter 6
The Ladybug's Plan

Before Zac and Pook had reached the bottom of the ridge, the Forest Creatures were back at the Linden stump, milling around, confused. A human caring for a tree is not what they expected. Ladybug flew to the platform atop the trunk. She gripped the mushroom podium. She spoke sternly. "Well, now! Don't you all feel foolish?"

Everyone was silent.

"It's Spider's fault!" blurted Firefly who slipped behind Bee, trying to avoid an angry stare from several of Spider's eyes.

Ladybug politely cleared her throat. She knew she had a tendency to scold. She wanted to be firm but polite. So she spoke slowly and calmly to the 'group' (as she called them). She reminded everyone that Dragonfly was good and brave. And that Spider was awfully cunning. And that they couldn't have come this far without everyone's help. But, she suggested, they must devise a new plan.

"You all saw how kind the human was to that tree. He seems strong, and he's even nice-looking, in a human sort of way. I believe there is a chance that the

And, though no vote was taken, the Ladybug
had become the new 'group' leader.

good human can help us to get rid of the evil human. But we all have to be willing—as a group—to ask for his help—and only if everyone in the group agrees . . ."

Everyone agreed—even Spider. And, though no vote was taken, the Ladybug had become the new 'group' leader.

Off they flew, in pursuit of Zac, with Grasshopper perched on Hummingbird's back, Ant riding on top of the Butterfly, Bee holding on to Snail, the Spider atop the Dragonfly and the heavy Caterpillar carried by both Firefly and Beetle. Ladybug led the way, flying alone.

Chapter 7
Ana

Although Ana had expected Zac to return several hours ago, she wasn't worried. Her husband could take care of himself in the Great Forest, and he had Pook to keep him company. Unlike other humans, Zac cared for the Forest—for the trees and other living things. Sometimes Ana wondered whether he might be a halfling like her with a human father and elf mother.

Yet Zac was human, and a handsome one too, and she knew he could have married any of the village girls—those stringy haired human females who giggled and flashed their beady eyes at him when he sold his boxes in the village. But Zac had married her, and she loved him with all her heart.

Ana didn't really mind when Zac left the house—it gave her a chance to clean up after the Fairies. Her Fairy friends provided great company, but they tricked and pestered everyone, human or halfling.

Her fairy friends provided great company,
but they tricked and pestered everyone,
human or halfling.

In this part of the Great Forest lived Flower Fairies, Kootenstoopits and Pickensrooters.

Ana's elf mother owned an ancient book titled, Ye Nomenclature of Faeries, from which she taught her halfling daughter the facts about her tiny half-cousins.

Ye Nomenclature of Faeries

Flower Faeries

Ye Flower Faeries be ye most friendlie and merrie of all ye Good People. Albeit they haveth wings of gossamer, they resemble elsewise smalle Humans. Of song and dancing they are right fond, and should one of them chance to whisper a tune in thy sleeping ear, that day long shalt thou hum the same without ceasing. Laughter also they love but it is said that of all Faerie Folk they are ye least mischievous; which is as well; for should they play on thee odd pranks or jests, thou woulds't never ken it, they being faster than ye know.

12

Kootenstoopits

Kootenstoopits be right short and chubby. They are eke called Urchins Spiggans and Dobies. Being of a solitary disposition, they do little harm. It is their want to try on all manner of shoes, howsoever bigge they might be: thus thou mayest from time to time hear them clumping about ye house. They seldom steal anything save buttons and socks.
These latter they believe do make especial good hats, which they wear on their heads and look right foolish thereby, and afterward lose them where no one can find.

Pickensrooters

Ye naughtiest of all ye Good Faeries be those knowne as Boggles, Spriggans or Pickensrooters. They seem to care not nor consider what they do. Wee man-like hands they have and rat-like tails; there is no lock they cannot pick nor bow of ribbon they cannot untie.

Verily they get into everything! They stop ye clocks, spill ye salt and steal ye victuals leftover. Moreover they putteth crumms in ye bed.

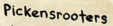

STADTHER 03

Ana lifted a Pickensrooter from a white cloud rising above a tin of flour on the kitchen counter. Between her long, elegant thumb and forefinger, she held the wriggling creature by its tail, and with a flick of the wrist, dispatched it out the open window. Yet, it didn't fall to the ground, but instead it beat its tiny wings and bobbed outside, as if it were on a string. Ana glared at the tiny creature as if she meant business, and it darted off.

She turned to clean up the spilled flour, pleased that she had caught the Pickensrooter before it made a bigger mess, when a sock—from which a pair of tiny feet protruded—scampered across the counter and smacked into the tin, spilling the flour everywhere. Ana knew that only a Kootenstoopit would do such a silly thing.

The flour-covered sock with the tiny protruding feet sat down on the counter, dazed. Ana pulled the sock off the tiny figure, and the Kootenstoopit smiled and waved up at her, completely proud of itself. It smiled so sweetly that Ana couldn't stay angry. So, she dusted off the sock, rolled it up tightly and placed it on the tiny fairy's head, so that the Kootenstoopit could see. Then she gently pushed the fairy out of the way, and began to clean up the mess.

Zac didn't even believe in Fairies.

As she swept, two glowing Flower Fairies appeared beside her delicately pointed ears and began to sing. Ana knew the song, and sang it with them.

By now, the sky beyond the kitchen had faded from blue to lavender, and Ana wondered what kept Zac. Was he all right? She closed her eyes and listened. She heard his thoughts. Yes, he was fine, and hurrying home as fast as the slow doth would let him.

Ana had inherited this gift from her mother. She could 'hear' Zac's thoughts whenever she liked. But try as she might, she had never been able to put thoughts into his head without speaking to him. After all, he was only human. Zac didn't even believe in Fairies. He had lived his whole life in the Forest and had never seen one. So he went on thinking that clocks merely stopped, buttons simply popped off, socks just disappeared because—well, because.

When Zac awoke beside Ana on their first married morning, he smiled at her explanation that Pickensrooters had tied his hair in knots, and that Kootenstoopits had scattered his clothes everywhere. He never found one of the socks he had lost that night—and they had been his favorite pair, light brown, with small tan rectangles.

It was almost dark now. Ana listened, and knew that Zac was close to home, carrying the heavy, trembling doth in his arms. Because he was Zac's friend, Ana loved Pook, too. Even if he was sometimes stinky.

Pook's name was an appropriate one—a tribute to his one unpleasant feature, especially after he had eaten too many purple thistles. Just before the stinky smell reached your nose, he would emit a little warning sound—pook!

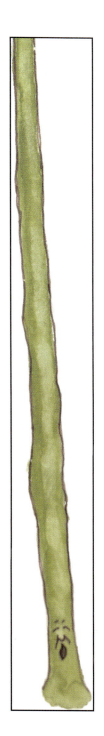

Just before the stinky smell reached your nose,
he would emit a little warning sound – pook!

Chapter 8
Yorah

he was the tallest and oldest tree in the Forest. By her own admission, she had "seen it all and done most of it, dearie!" Yorah called everyone "dearie" or "sweetie"—partly because she couldn't see as well as she used to, and couldn't always recognize her partners in conversation.

Wise from centuries of life, what she hadn't learned from being the tallest tree in the Forest, she had been taught by the forest creatures that landed in her branches. She sometimes spoke a little too frankly, but always truthfully—except on the subject of her own failing eyesight. She didn't want anyone to know she was growing old. After all, there were still some strong young oaks she wouldn't mind getting to know . . .

Yorah had raised thousands of oak trees from acorns. You might say that she had raised Ana too. After her mother died, Ana had grown up in the shelter of Yorah's spreading limbs. There, Ana became friendly with the Fairies who she first saw singing in Yorah's branches and dancing among Yorah's roots. And there, Zac first saw Ana—he had been looking for timber, but found instead a lovely halfling girl singing alone in the Forest. And so, it was in Yorah's shade that

She was the tallest and oldest tree in the Forest

Zac and Ana met everyday. He proposed there. And he built their home there—not under the tree, but in it.

A delicate-looking but sturdy walnut staircase spiraled around the trunk of the oak tree, up to the central room. The other rooms—bedroom, kitchen and workshop—perched like nests, on different limbs of the tree, connected to the center room by rope bridges.

"Your husband's out late tonight, isn't he dearie?"

"Don't worry Yorah—he's nearly home."

"Really? I can't see him yet. Nothing wrong with my vision, mind you, sweetie, it's just the dark."

"Of course, Yorah."

Ana's heart jumped when she heard Zac's boots on the stairs. As he entered the room, she rushed to kiss him—a warm, slow, tomorrow-is-our-first-anniversary kiss. Zac dropped the birch limb from under his left arm and pulled her closer. Pook, under Zac's right arm, raised his head, smiled, and waited for his kiss, too.

Ana bent and kissed him on the top of his broad head. "Hello, stinky doth," she said.

"What about me? Aren't you going to say 'hello' to your husband?"

Ana smiled and touched a finger to the tip of his chin. "Okay. Hello, stinky human."

Chapter 9
The Jewelry Box

As Ana and Pook slept, Zac sat at his workbench completing his anniversary present. Zac loved his workshop and he loved his work. Here he shaped carefully selected hardwoods, scraped and sanded and joined them and finished them with stain and varnish. Before him, in orderly array, lay his woodworking tools—rasps, chisels, and planes. On the wall behind him hung the timbering tools he hadn't used in months—spoke shaves, mallets and saws. The area where he used to stack wood remained empty.

Zac's father had taught him the craft of wood working: the secrets of dovetail joints, cross-lapped joints, mortise and tenon joints; how to grind and hone a blunt chisel; how to inlay wood and carve a relief; how to age the varnish which could give blond maple a rich and dark sheen; and the types of wood— cherry, elm, walnut, smooth beech, with its easy to carve pale grain, and silver birch, with its creamy white sap wood and pale brown heart wood.

Zac stripped the bark from the edges of the birch limb and split it. The two perfectly matched halves would complete the top of Ana's jewel box. He was hunched over, planing the wood smooth, when the embassy of Forest Creatures, led by Ladybug, arrived and perched on a branch in the workshop.

After reminding the others to behave, Ladybug hopped in and landed on the end of the workbench. She stood straight, coughed softly, and began her first conversation with a human.

"Large sir. On behalf of the visiting delegation, permit me to introduce myself."

Out of the corner of his eye, Zac noticed the tiny creature. Since he had seen few living things, even insects, in this part of the Forest for some time, and because he was happy to have late-night company, he smiled at her.

Certain she had his attention now, Ladybug continued. "Please pardon our interruption of your doubtless important labors, but I have come on a mission of even greater importance . . ."

She realized that the human was once more bent over his work, and was ignoring her completely.

"Oh dear," she said, turning to the group in the window. "What do we do now? He is deaf."

"He's not deaf, silly" said Butterfly. "Your voice is too small for him to hear. Maybe if I fly up close to his

49

ear . . ."

"No," said Ladybug. "You're right. We need someone with a much bigger voice than either of ours.
How about Hummingbird?"

"Are you nuts?" said Beetle. "Hummingbirds
don't know any words. That's why they hum."

"Mayhap the human is unfamiliar with contem-
porary bug 'vo-cab-u-lar-y'," observed the scholarly
Caterpillar.

"I . . . Would. . . Be . . ." began Snail—but he
always spoke so slowly that everyone, as usual, paid no
attention to him.

"Bee's loud," said Beetle. "Bee? Give it a try."

"I'll zzzzpeak to him," buzzed Bee. "My
pleazzzure."

He began to make buzzing zig zag orbits around
Zac's head, performing the intricate airborne dance by
which all bees communicate. Zac, irritated, shooed
him away. Bee returned to the others.

"Hizzz hearing izzz fine," he reported. "He'zz
juzzzt zzztupid."

Meanwhile, Snail continued, "Happy. . . To. . .
Speak . . ."

"My turn," said Firefly. "Everyone stand back."
He ascended to the center of the open window and,
with the night sky for a background, flashed a message
about the evil Blight-Spreader and the threat to the
Forest. Zac, concentrating hard now as he sanded the
final corner of the box lid, never even looked up at

him.

Firefly gave up. "This human is not only deaf and stupid. He's blind."

"Now we eat him," whispered Spider.

Snail concluded his oration, addressing no one, "To. . . Him."

"Hush, all of you!" said the exasperated Ladybug. "Just because the human seems to have a problem understanding . . ."

"A problem?" said Ant, acidly. "I've lived in stumps that were smarter than him."

Unaware of the commotion outside his window, Zac lovingly rubbed the box with tung oil. It was the finest, most beautiful box he had ever made, and he had finished it in time. It was almost midnight.

He blew out the workshop lamps and silently crossed the swinging bridge to the bedroom. After tucking the present under the bed, he joined Ana and Pook under the covers.

As he drifted to sleep, Ana sighed and turned and held him so close that he could almost hear her dreams.

Chapter 10
Yorah Understands

O utside the workshop, high above the disappointed delegation of Forest Creatures, the leaves of the tall oak tree rustled.

"Oh my," said Ladybug. "How rude of us not to have greeted you, Madam Oak."

"Not a problem, honey. But you speak so softly. Fly a little closer so I can see—ah, that is—hear you better."

Ladybug flew up to the tip of Yorah's nose—so that Yorah had to cross her eyes to keep her in focus. "Can you hear me now?"

she shouted.

"Well. Aren't you as cute as a bug?" Yorah cackled at her own joke.

The blushing Ladybug formally introduced each member of "our little group," and tactfully explained the difficulty they had experienced in attempting to communicate with the human who lived in her branches.

"He isn't deaf, sweetie. But his head is harder than the ironwood he carves. He's stubborn. Hard headed. Why, he doesn't even believe in Fairies."

"I told you he wazz zzztupid," said Bee.

"That does it—let's eat him while he's sleeping," said Spider.

"How does he think the world works?" asked the astonished Ladybug. "Does he think everything happens by accident?"

"He has a good heart," said Yorah, "but he's the kind of man humans call 'practical'." But maybe I can help you, sweeties. I have my ways, you know. What seems to be the problem?"

As Ladybug and the others began to explain why they had come to Zac, it became clear—by the way Yorah gasped and trembled in shock—that all of this—the dark dust, the Blight-Spreader, the Forest Creatures he crystallized and collected—was news to her. Because of her failing vision, the oldest and wisest of trees had been blissfully unaware that the Great Forest was dying around her!

Not that she admitted a thing. "Yes, of course."
"Naturally." "Uh-huh." "I see." were all she said. But
now Yorah understood, and for the first time in her
long life, she feared the danger.

She didn't show it, of course. "Not to worry,
critters," she said. "I'll take care of it. Now it's time all
of you got some rest." And she invited them all to
spend the night in the safety of her branches.

Up they flew, with Ladybug leading the way.

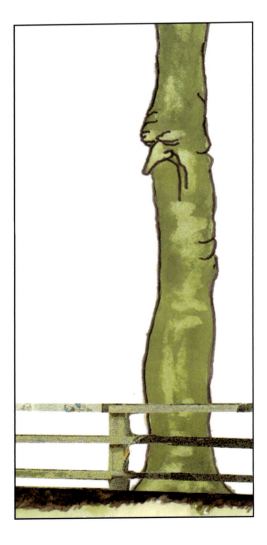

Chapter 11
Rusful

The grotto, once the most beautiful place in the Forest, led to a silent underground palace with long, deep passages and vaulted chambers, all cut within the limestone hill by millions of years of rain.

Once, a clear stream had spilled from the grotto's mouth and splashed over pale rocks into the valley below.

Now, the stream oozed and bubbled, thick with the dark dust and a foul-smelling slime that stuck to everything it touched. Where it collected into stagnant pools, it sent up sulfurous wisps of vapor. Its banks were black—as if the very rocks had been scorched.

Deep inside the acrid grotto, the dimly lit walls appeared to move. On every ledge and in every crevasse writhing black forms—the Darklings—so densely crammed, that when one of them moved, it sent a ripple through the others.

Still deeper inside, in the center of an even darker chamber, perched on a blunt stalagmite, sat a human figure—at least, in the dim light, it resembled a human, with arms, legs and a head directly between its shoulders. If you dared risk a closer inspection, you would see that its four thin limbs jutted out at awkward angles, and that the skin of its hideous mottled face appeared to boil. This was the one the Forest Creatures called the Blight-Spreader. He was Rusful, Master of the Darklings.

The Darklings could scarcely remember a time when he had not ruled over them, although not so very long ago, Rusful had been the village apothecary—useful but not liked, gray, taciturn and grasping. By day, he had grudgingly mixed medicines and sold them dearly to the villagers. But by night, he employed a deep study of the earth's elements to transmute lead into gold. And, like every alchemist before and since, he failed. But he had stumbled, by accident, onto an even more powerful and dangerous concoction—a lethal poison that transformed living things into precious jewels.

As he perfected his wicked formula, Rusful had accidentally contaminated himself with it. His body became distorted. His skin erupted, and he became fatally sensitive to sunlight.

Ashamed, and angered by his shame, he had fled from the village by night and wandered through the Forest until he found the grotto. There he encountered the Darklings—ugly, malevolent fairies sometimes known to humans as Skrileers, Yarthkins and Wraiths. Rusful first formed an alliance with them and was soon acclaimed their Master. Combining his science with their magic, he finally created the dark dust which turned living things into precious jewels, and together they began to destroy the living Forest.

Soon, he had lined the walls of his dank chamber with the branches of dead trees from which he hung his gleaming collection of jeweled Forest Creatures.

Now he rose from his cold throne and the Darklings left their perches to gather around him. From a pocket in his filthy laboratory coat, Rusful produced a leather pouch. They saw it, and moaned hungrily. With one hand he tipped the pouch, slowly sifting a heap of ash black powder into his other palm. The jostling crowd surged around his knees, straining, grasping, and whimpering for a taste of the dark dust.

"Not yet darlings," he teased, holding the pouch high. "First, we have work to do." The writhing mob parted as he pushed through them like the bow of a rusty ship plowing through an oily sea.

At the very mouth of the grotto he stood, and as the Darklings gathered around him, Rusful stepped out into the emptiness. They caught him, and rose with him into the sky. Bearing Rusful, the Blight-Spreader, they swarmed into the night.

Chapter 12
Yorah's Plan

orah shook her branches— slowly at first, then forcefully, as if she were announcing a change in the weather. In their sleep, Zac and Ana dreamt of an approaching storm. The various

Fairies dropped whatever mischief they were up to and listened.

The oak called them, and they rushed to the center room and waited for her to speak.

Pook, at the foot of Zac and Ana's bed with his head stuck out of the covers, blinked awake. He had heard something. Instinctively he sucked in air, preparing to let loose a volley of blood-curdling barks. He held his breath but he could not bark. Anyway, it was silent now. If it were something, it had probably gone away so it might be safe to take a look around.

The doth dropped off the bed with a thump, left the bedroom and crept—backwards, so nothing could sneak up on him—across the swinging bridge to the center room. And tripped over several Fairies.

"Shhhh, you clumsy doth" they whispered. "Sit down and listen."

Pook had glimpsed Fairies from time to time, but he had never seen so many gathered together. It confused him—and when he was confused, he kept his mouth shut. The Fairies seemed to be staring at a knothole in the trunk of the oak, so Pook stared too. To his amazement, the knothole began to change, slowly transforming into a kind, old face. "Hello dearies," said the face.

Pook's ears shot up. Zac had been telling the truth! Trees could talk!

"As you all know, nothing happens in the Great Forest that escapes this old gal's attention," Yorah said. The considerate Fairies suppressed their giggles. "I haven't spoken to you about it before, because I didn't want to upset you. However, the time has come for action." And she proceeded to tell them about the evil Blight-Spreader, the dark dust and the Forest Creatures crystallized into jewels.

"I have a plan," Yorah said. "But it must be carried out tonight. I am giving you a very important task. Not a difficult one, but I must tell you that it might be dangerous."

Several of the Kootenstoopits stuck their fingers in their ears, because they didn't want to hear about anything that wasn't fun.

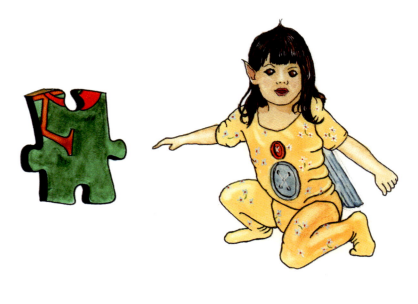

As simply as she could, Yorah explained their mission, emphasizing that it must be completed before sunrise. She knew she could trust the Flower Fairies and Pickensrooters. She told the Kootenstoopits just stay out of the way, then she wished them luck and reminded them that she loved them.

The Fairies disappeared. Pook found himself sitting alone in the dark, empty room, staring at a knothole. He tucked in his wings and returned to his warm, safe spot at the foot of Zac and Ana's bed.

Chapter 13
The Theft

Darklings and Rusful were far away and high over the Forest when the Fairies arrived at the grotto.

They flew in, their glowing bodies lighting the halls, and entered Rusful's cavern. It was empty, except for the pots, cauldrons and retorts that the evil one used to brew his potions, and the dead trees hung with jeweled Forest Creatures.

The Fairies instantly began to do what they did best—they made a mess.

Like sparks that fly upward from a bonfire, they sped, flickering, in all directions. But each Fairy had a precise destination. Pickensrooters seized and smashed vials of fluids against the cavern walls and spilled cauldrons of dark dust into the stream (taking very special care not to touch the dust), while Flower Fairies darted among the trees gathering up the jewels that Rusful had hung on the petrified branches.

The Kootenstoopits, who had been warned by Yorah not to do anything at all, sat on the floor and played with bits of the alchemist's tools—copper coils, cork stoppers and shiny glass containers. These they particularly enjoyed, making faces at their own reflections in the glass. Then, one of the silly creatures, after a long session of putting on, adjusting and taking off his sock hat, suddenly lost interest in his appearance and (unfortunately) stuffed the sock into a small crevasse in the floor near Rusful's work area.

Well before sunrise, with the evil laboratory wrecked, the last beaker broken and all the poison spilled, the Fairies turned and fled, with the stolen jewels in their arms.

It had been a good night of mischief. Yorah would be pleased.

Chapter 14
Rusful's Return

There was a pale morning light teasing the horizon as the Darkling swarm approached the grotto. Rusful urged them to fly faster. Only when they lowered him to the ground, did he notice the change in the stream. It appeared to be frozen, protruding from the grotto's mouth like a leprous black tongue. Moaning, the Blight-Spreader stumbled as fast as his skewed legs would permit through the cavernous passageways, and beheld, in his chamber, the scene of destruction. He howled and writhed, twisting his awkward arms around his misshapen body as if wringing out a wet rag. "My work destroyed! My jewels stolen!"

Outside the laboratory-cavern, the Darklings crouched and trembled. Within, Rusful slumped on the flat stalagmite that was his throne and surveyed the wreckage. Every vial was shattered, every cauldron spilled, all his potions and powders emptied into the now polluted stream. Worse, his precious collection was gone—every single jewel. Who had done this?

Dejected, he stumbled through the debris. Splinters of glass crunched under his shoes. He bowed his head in despair. And then he saw it.

"A sock?"

Painfully, he stooped and then straightened, holding the sock close to his red, watery eyes. He rubbed it between his yellow fingers, as if he were back in the village, selecting material for a new shirt. What did this have to do with his missing jewels? He remembered reading somewhere that certain Fairies enjoyed playing with such stupid things . . .

Then the truth struck him. Of course! Fairies! The thieves were Fairies!

A colony of them, he remembered, infested that tall old oak tree on the far side of the Forest, sharing it with a common woodcarver and his halfling mate. Rusful screamed a command to his leather-winged subjects to assemble. He gave his orders.

The Darklings swarmed up from the grotto,
headed for the oak tree, like a storm cloud, terrible
against the dawn sky.

Chapter 15
The Anniversary

heir mission
completed,
the tired Fairies
hovered over
the sleeping old
oak and the
many sleepers she sheltered.

Yorah had given them no instructions
about what to do with the jewels, but they all
agreed that the best thing to do with anything one finds was to hide it. And they

knew the ideal place. The jewels fit perfectly in the twelve compartments of the box under the bed. No one would think to look for them there!

The box closed with a click as the Fairies vanished. The sound disturbed Zac's sleep.

Something told him that morning had arrived—the morning of his anniversary. Ana, his bride of exactly one year, lay warm on his arm. Without opening his eyes, he turned and held her, nuzzled her hair, and kissed her.

Ana did not, at that moment, share her husband's tender feelings. She sat instead on the edge of the bed brushing her hair, watching Zac plant a long kiss on the face of the delighted Pook, who had just now wriggled up from his place at the foot.

She spoke loudly enough to awaken her husband. "Maybe I should leave the two of you alone."

Zac opened his eyes in time to receive Pook's return kiss—a long wet lick, from his chin to his forehead. Wide awake he realized his chance to avenge Ana's calling him a 'stinky human'. He grinned. He cuddled Pook lovingly and announced, "You look especially lovely today, my darling." Pook played his part, batting his eyes coyly.

"I wish I could say the same about you," purred Ana.

Ow. Got me again, Zac thought. It's hard to

outsmart a halfling.

Ana, laughing, threw her arms around him and kissed him. "Happy Anniversary," she whispered, and kissed him again—then stopped and drew back, wrinkling her nose.

"Ugh. Time to get rid of the doth."

Once more, Pook had lived up to his name and reputation.

She set the fat doth firmly on the floor and retrieved something from under the bed. It was obviously a chisel, poorly disguised in tissue wrapping. "Your present," she said. "I hope you can use it." Zac, who truly hadn't expected a gift, tore open the package and acted suitably surprised at the contents.

Now, from under his side of the bed, he produced the box, and shyly presented it. Ana gasped, and held it in her lap. It was wonderful, and more wonderful because Zac had made it for her.

"Is it just as beautiful inside?" she asked him.

"Shall I open it?"

"Of course." Her husband, proud of his handiwork, only wished it were filled with the jewels she deserved.

He saw her eyes widen as she looked inside. She caught her breath. "Oh, Zac!"

He stole a peek, and gasped. Where had those jewels come from? How did they get into the box? Should he tell Ana he didn't know? Of all the strange things that had happened in his year of marriage to Ana, this was by far the strangest.

"They're so beautiful," she said, her eyes filling with tears. "How . . . why . . ."

Zac thought he should take a lesson from Pook—when confused, keep your mouth shut.

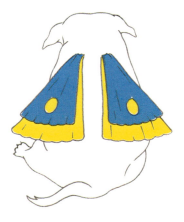

Chapter 16
The Jewels are Hidden in the Forest

Pook always enjoyed his morning walk with Zac as they looked for wood. Ana blew them a kiss as they set out. Over her head, in Yorah's branches, the Forest Creatures began to awaken.

Keen-eyed, but speechless, Hummingbird first saw the Darkling cloud on the horizon. Hovering in front of the drowsy Group Leader, she beat her wings frantically and jerked her head up and down, pointing with her beak toward the sky. "Yes dear, I can see that it's a nice day," yawned Ladybug.

At that moment, the dozing Dragonfly awoke. He saw the cloud, too, and instantly assumed his Air Group leader role, shouting, "Condition Red! Battle stations!"

High in the branches of the tall oak, one by one the Forest Creatures blinked awake and watched the ominous swarm as it drew nearer.

They might have panicked but Ladybug took command. They could, she pointed out, expect no help from the strong human man, who seemed to be away from the tree house. But she hoped the group would agree that Yorah had to be informed, immedi-

73

ately. For once, she decided against being polite. "Madam Oak," shouted Ladybug. "I know you can't see it yet, but I must tell you that an army of Darklings is headed this way."

The news stunned Yorah. Obviously, something had gone terribly wrong with her plan. Somehow, she had put her beloved Ana in harm's way, and now she had to warn her. She struggled to keep the fear out of her voice as she whispered through the knothole in the bedroom, "Good morning, Ana dear."

"Good anniversary morning, you mean. Look. Aren't they wonderful?" She held up the glittering jewels for Yorah to see. "I can't believe Zac gave them to me."

"Actually, I don't think he can believe it either, sweetie."

By now, even Yorah could dimly make out the enormous threatening shadow descending through the bright morning sky. "Ana, I have something important to tell you but there's no time for words—you will have to listen to my thoughts."

Ana closed her eyes. Instantly she knew almost everything—how the jewels had come into her possession, how Yorah's plan to save the Forest had gone wrong, and that the Darklings were on their way to reclaim Rusful's precious collection.

The daughters of Elves don't frighten easily.

"Yorah, I know that the Blight-Spreader is evil,"

74

Ana answered. "But if these jewels belong to him, I'll simply give them back."

Only then did the Yorah tell her the true nature of those jewels, which she thought so beautiful—that they were once living creatures that had been crystallized by the cruel and greedy Rusful.

Now the shadow of the Darkling swarm fell over the tree, and the air was full of a stench like sulfur. Ana could hear the scratching of claws among branches above her. She made up her mind.

Ana summoned her Fairies who instantly appeared around her. Ana pressed the jewels into their hands and without saying a word she issued instructions. The jewels must be hidden in the Forest where the Blight-Spreader could not find them. They understood. And the Fairies and the jewels vanished just before the first of the grinning, leering Darklings entered her bedroom.

Darklings hated and feared elves. Only because Ana was half-human, did they dare approach her. Ana crossed her arms over her chest and spoke coldly to them. "Get out of my house, you filthy beasts."

They hesitated, hissing and grumbling, looking away from her threatening gaze. But as more filled the room, those nearest her pressed closer. Their foul smell was overpowering. Their slippery wings pushed against her legs. Their dirty hands tugged at the hem of her dress.

In the branches high above her head, the Forest Creatures cowered, helpless. The leaves that hid them, where the Darklings had brushed against the old oak, were withering, mottled black.

Ana knew that Rusful's raiding horde had come for the jewels but she did not guess what they would take instead—until two Darklings stood by her side. Abruptly, as if obeying a command, the pair seized her hands and stretched her arms wide.

Then, the entire swarm surrounded her, lifted her, and carried her from her home, high over Yorah and the trembling creatures, away over the dying Forest toward the grotto.

Then, the entire swarm surrounded her,
and carried her from her home,...

Chapter 17
The Hostage

Rusful sat clutching his head, pinching and rubbing it as if it were a bumpy round gourd for sale from a dubious grocer. He stared at the terrified Ana as the Darklings brought her in, stood and coldly sneered, "A halfling?"

"Let go of me, you hideous monsters," Ana said, and for a moment managed to wriggle free of her captors' cold clutches.

Rusful howled and waved his arms over his

head like thin ropes. "You bring me a halfling? Fools! Traitors! What can I do with a halfling? Where are my jewels?"

"Jewels? What jewels?" asked Ana, innocently. She heard Rusful's thoughts. She sensed the terrible greed that consumed him, and knew that he would stop at nothing to get the jewels back.

But Ana sensed something else in the cold, writhing mind of the Blight-Spreader—fear. Rusful feared something, something he hated—something outside of the dark grotto.

Her Darkling captors took hold of her again, and thrust her toward their Master. Rusful extended his long, yellow index finger so that it almost touched Ana's forehead. He held it there, considering what to do next. He wondered if he should kill her; infect her with a fatal touch. But just possibly, this kidnapped halfling knew something about the Fairies who had wrecked his work and stolen his jewels.

"I know you" Rusful said. "You live in that big oak tree with the woodcarver.

Does he have my jewels?"

Ana flared. "He has nothing to do with this. You leave Zac alone."

Rusful leaned closer. "Precious to you is he? Are you precious to him I wonder? I am a collector of precious things."

Her head ached. She could feel the power of his greed, hear his wretched mind twisting, grasping with need.

"No," he said. "Of course he doesn't have them.

He stared at the terrified Ana as the Darklings brought her in,
stood and coldly sneered, "A halfling?"

You gave them to the Fairies, didn't you?"

"If the Fairies had them," she said, "they would become bored with them and leave them scattered around in broad daylight, wouldn't they? Why don't you go look for them yourself?"

At the word daylight, Rusful moaned, and his face clenched. Ana understood more. He feared the sun. She knew now that sunlight would kill him. Exposed to the sun, poisoned by his own potions, he would turn to stone, just like the trees and Forest Creatures! But she also knew now that his slightest touch would poison her.

Rusful's finger hovered inches from her eyes. He glared, then suddenly screamed in her face, "Where are my jewels?"

"You won't find out from me," she said.

Something resembling a smile twisted his dreadful face. He had devised a plan, and Ana knew it immediately. She fought back tears.

He summoned a team of Darklings. "Put the Halfling there," he ordered, pointing to the row of dead and dying trees lining the cavern walls. One of them, a broken and hollow willow, only touched with blight, with strong branches growing outward from its base and meeting again at its top, would become Ana's prison.

She struggled as the Darklings picked her up and

carried her to it. "Let me go!"

"Let you go?" mocked Rusful. "If I let you go, how shall I have my precious jewels again?"

"The jewels are hidden in the forest, where you can't find them."

"I can't?" Rusful laughed. "No. But your husband can. If you really are precious to him, he will find them for me, and bring them to me, and put them in my hands."

Ana pulled at the cage of willow branches. "I've told you. My husband doesn't know where the jewels are hidden."

"Perhaps not. Not yet. But I know that you Elves and Halflings have a way of speaking without words. You will think where they are hidden, and he will hear your thoughts, and bring my jewels to me."

Defeated, Ana wept. "He can't hear me. I can't do it," she sobbed.

"Ah, but you will," he answered. "And soon."

He produced the leather pouch, shook out a handful of the dark dust and scattered it at the base of the willow tree.

"Within a fortnight that tree that holds you will turn to stone. And so, my dear, will you."

Within a fortnight that tree that holds you
will turn to stone. And so my dear, will you.

The Dream

As usual, it was almost dark as Zac and Pook returned to their home in the big oak tree after spending another fruitless day looking for wood. And, once again, Pook, tucked under Zac's arm, trembled and grunted at the thought of the approaching darkness.

Zac bounded up the long tree house staircase and, as he entered the center room, felt the hair rise on the back of his neck. The house felt empty.

Something or someone was missing. The usually happy home was silent. Now, he heard only the sound of his boots echoing as he walked through the empty house.

Pook, too, sensed something bad had happened and he trembled even more. With his head held low and his wings tucked down by his portly body, he followed Zac into the bedroom, scooted up behind Zac's boots and peered around in front of Zac hoping that he would not see anything bad.

The bedroom, torn asunder, stank a foul stench. It showed the struggle that had taken place there. The jewelry box, once filled with those mysterious jewels, lay askew on the bed, empty.

Zac could only guess at what had become of his wife and the jewels but he knew it was not good. And he knew he had to find her.

He grabbed the shaking doth with one hand and

his broad axe with the other and headed down the staircase. Whatever had taken his beautiful wife would pay. And he would find her even if he had to search the entire Great Forest.

Zac ran through the Great Forest calling for Ana, he tore at the branches and vines that hung in his path to find her, but to no avail. Pook struggled to keep up—afraid to lag behind and too loyal to flee.

Soon, it was very dark and they were deep in the Forest. It was well past midnight and they were too tired to continue. Zac's head ached as he rested against a large tree. He pulled the grunting Pook close to him. Zac closed his eyes and tried to hear Ana's thoughts. He knew that she could tell him where she was. She could lead him to her captor—if only he could hear her thoughts. But he never had heard her thoughts before and he couldn't hear them now. If only he had paid more attention then perhaps he could find her—but he hadn't—and now, she paid for his hard headedness.

As he lay against the tree, his breathing slowed and his mind began to drift to thoughts of his wife and how she always sang to him. Soon, he began to sleep—and dream.

He dreamt of trees standing side by side within a mist and rising from the mist, in the center of the strands of trees, was the face of his wife. She held her arms out to him but he could not reach her. She opened her mouth to speak but he could not hear her. And, as her image floated above him, he began to hear singing. The singing seemed to come from the trees —— from knotholes in the trees. And, the knotholes moved like mouths, singing to him: "Moon like, moon like. Dreamer one on ending, I cause your puzzling." They repeated the song over and over as if trying to tell him something that he could not understand.

Then, the mist changed. It swirled and coalesced and rose in the sky. The mist rose higher and higher until it disappeared into a hole in the sky. And then, from the hole, shone a bright light directly onto the sleeping Pook. And, in Zac's dream, Pook became one of the beautiful but lifeless crystals like the Jewels that had once been in Ana's jewelry box.

Then, the dream changed again. Gone were the trees and the night sky and Zac stood at the mouth of a dark grotto. Before him lay an open box that was as long as it was wide and inside the box were smaller boxes arranged in rows, five to a side.

Suddenly, the sky shone as bright as day, and Zac could see the Great Forest more clearly than he had ever seen it before and he looked at the Forest in a new way. He could see things that he had never seen before and he took those things and filled the small boxes with them. He now knew what to do to get Ana back. He knew where the jewels were hidden and he knew he had to exchange them for his wife. And he would find them before noon tomorrow.

Chapter 18
The Ransom

t was high noon as Zac and Pook
approached the blackened boulders
under the hill with the jewels that
Zac had found, but it had grown dark
from the approaching storm. Both
man and doth looked up at the iron-
gray sky and shuddered. As they began the hard climb,
Pook stayed close to Zac's boots. From time to time,
Pook paused and looked back, torn between his loyalty
to Zac and his overwhelming urge to retreat down to
the valley.

Zac boosted the scrambling Pook over a huge,
blight-covered rock, climbed up after him and
dropped to the ground. There, he could see the grotto—the doorway to the underworld, a shapeless black
hole in the mountain, gaping like the mouth of a
corpse. As in his dreams, the moment he saw it, Zac
heard a growl of thunder.

He stared, summoning up the courage to enter.
Behind him, Pook crouched and trembled, expecting
something to jump at him out of the darkness. Then
they both saw something move, a darker shadow
among the shadows. Pook closed his eyes. In a lifetime
of timidity, he had never wanted more to run away.

Zac gasped as he saw what appeared to be a yel-

88

low finger, floating in the darkness of the grotto, a thin deformed one, scaly and ulcerous. Zac assumed that the hideous digit must belong to a similarly hideous person. The finger twitched, beckoning.

"Come in," said someone.

Zac, startled by the voice, answered bravely, "No. You come out."

Silence.

Although Pook wanted desperately to fly, to get far away from the dark cave and the thing in the cave, he froze with fear. The darkness around him deepened as the clouds overhead thickened.

Zac spoke. "Who are you?"

"Give me my jewels!" the thing in darkness moaned.

In the gloom inside the grotto, Zac could now make out a gnarled hand, held open.

"I propose a fair trade," said the voice. "You give me my jewels; I give you your wife."

Zac's anger flared. "Bring my wife to me now, or I'll rip you apart!"

If the person in the shadows replied, Zac couldn't hear, for a long roll of thunder boomed overhead and echoed through the valley. The hand disappeared.

Zac shouted, desperately, "Wait! Come back! I'll give you your jewels! Here they are. Here, take them."

The hand, visible again, waited.

In Rusful's chamber, in her prison of willow, Ana could sense Zac's presence. She concentrated her thoughts on him. "Don't trust him, Zac. Don't give up the jewels. Lure him out into the sunlight somehow. Please, please my darling be careful not to touch him." But she knew he couldn't hear her.

Pook opened his eyes. The thing-in-the-dark hadn't gone away. He wanted to snarl, to bark, to frighten the bad thing away. He opened his mouth, but couldn't even manage one "uff." Pook had never been more afraid.

Holding the jewels in both his hands, Zac took a step closer to the grotto. Rusful's hand reached out of the darkness. They were almost close enough to touch.

Pook's ears stood up. Something—someone— was telling him his best friend Zac was in mortal danger!

Far away, Yorah could feel the storm approaching. Her branches tossed and swayed. The Fairies and Forest Creatures who she sheltered huddled together.

As more thunder rumbled, a flickering shaft of sunlight suddenly pierced the clouds and struck the jewels, making them sparkle and glitter—as if Zac held a handful of stars.

Rusful cupped his hand to receive the jewels. His long yellow fingers wriggled, taunting, greedy. Zac's anger finally exploded and he tossed the jewels in the air. As his enemy reached for them, Zac intended to yank him from his filthy cave and rip him to pieces. And when Rusful's bony wrist appeared, Zac's hand shot out to seize it.

Pook knew something was very wrong. He wasn't going to let his best friend die. It was at this very moment that he snarled and leapt.

The force of his wing-beating attack knocked Zac sideways and down to his knees. Above him, he saw Pook's teeth flash white, saw Pook's powerful jaws clamp down on Rusful's arm pulling him out of the grotto.

With the evil Rusful out of the entrance of the grotto, Zac scrambled to his feet and ran, stumbling and shouting Ana's name, through the echoing stone passages of the cave and into the pitch-black cavern. He could see nothing. He could hear only his own harsh breathing and the blood pounding in his temples. And then, wonderfully, he heard Ana's voice. "Zac, I'm here."

He ran blindly to the sound, reaching out. His hand touched the willow stump then Ana's hand. He tore furiously at the willow limbs, bending and breaking them, releasing his wife from prison, and held her in his arms.

Hand in hand, exhausted, triumphant, Zac and Ana emerged from the grotto—and there they saw the aftermath of Pook's fierce battle with the Blight-Spreader.

The struggle had been brief. Pook had pulled Rusful out of the grotto's mouth, and together they had fallen, tangled and thrashing, into the brightness of the one beam of sunlight still piercing the clouds. But, it had been enough.

Now, Rusful's petrified remains—a broken heap of glistening black rocks, scarcely recognizable as a human form, with one grasping hand outstretched—lay on the ground. Beside Rusful stood Pook's small, crystallized body. Around the two lifeless bodies lay the twelve shining jewels, scattered where they had fallen.

Stunned, speechless with grief, Ana and Zac stood and stared. They hadn't expected this. Pook wasn't supposed to die.

Zac sank to his knees beside his lifeless friend and touched him gently. "Why?" He said tenderly, as if Pook could hear him. "Why were you so brave today? I could have saved Ana. You didn't have to die."

But Ana understood. "He saved your life, Zac. If you had so much as touched that monster, you would have been the one turned to stone. I tried to warn you, but you couldn't hear my thoughts."

"Pook must have heard you," said Zac.

Zac put his arms around Pook's cold, hard little body. The words caught in his throat. "Thank you, Pook. Good boy." Ana knelt beside Pook and kissed his broad head, half expecting him to lean back and smile at her. But Pook's sweet face was frozen in a ferocious snarl. Timid in life, he would forever look brave in death.

Timid in life, he would forever look brave in death.

Chapter 19
The Rain

The air was heavy, still and misty. A few cool raindrops joined the warm tears on Ana's face. "Goodbye, dear stinky doth," Ana whispered, and hugged Pook for the last time.

Zac and Ana left Pook and the jewels and began their long walk home down the blackened mountain, through the ruined Forest. As they walked, it began to rain harder than it ever had before.

Zac and Ana arrived at the tree house near midnight and they could not have been any wetter. In the Forest, the rain continued to fall harder and harder.

Zac carried Ana up the stairs to the center room. He shuddered, numb with cold and grief. Ana shivered against his shoulder and sobbed, tears streaming from her eyes as rainwater streamed from her hair. After a while, as he held her, Ana drifted into a light sleep. Above them, all around them, the rain poured and a gentle wind stirred the great oak's leaves.

"I love you, too," Zac said.

Ana stirred, and opened her almond shaped eyes. "Too? I didn't say anything, Zac. I just thought it."

Then—in a rush, as if dawn had broken bright as noon—all of Ana's thoughts filled Zac's mind. He understood not only her love for him, and grief for Pook, but also her conversations with Yorah, what had become of the lost buttons and missing socks—and the Fairies. He now knew that the Fairies were real.

And now that he believed in them—he could see them.

They were everywhere. Hundreds of them, some small and silly, others bright and beautiful. Some glowed and hovered. Some sat and played with their toes. Many wept and comforted each other in their grief for the lost Pook.

Then Yorah spoke, and for the first time, Zac could hear her—a grandmother tucking in a pair of over-tired children. "Go to sleep now, the two of you. Things are always better in the morning."

For once, Ana thought, Yorah was wrong. But she obediently took Zac's hand and led him to bed. That night they slept holding each other close and, while the storm poured down into the Great Forest, they heard each other's dreams.

Chapter 20
The Great Forest

The morning sky shone like a recently washed saucer. Where the Forest Creatures slept, Yorah's green leaves trembled and tossed in a fresh, cool breeze. Caterpillar snored softly in his small silk tent. Beetle lay on his back, his feet twitching in the air. At dawn, even the tired sentry Firefly had extinguished his taillight and gone to sleep. Only Spider was awake. Planning.

She had attached a single strand of web to a twig and was silently inching down it toward the face of deeply sleeping Zac.

Snail awoke, and saw Spider. As fast as he could—which was none too fast—he spoke.

"Uh. . . Oh. Everybody. . . Get. . .Up."

Spider continued her relentless descent. She hung just above Zac's nose.

Snail shouted. "Spider . . . Is . . . Going . . ."

Ladybug, on the leaf nearest to Snail's, stirred in her sleep.

Snail, in a panic, went on. "To . . . Eat . . ."

Instantly, Ant awoke. "Eat? Yes! Eat what? Where's breakfast?"

That did it. Everyone was up now. Hummingbird hummed hungrily. "Izzz there honey?" buzzed Bee.

"Oh dear!" shrieked Ladybug.

"The . . . human," Snail concluded, with a slow sigh of relief.

Spider climbed on her strand of web so near to Zac that she swayed with his every breath, and the tips of her legs brushed his nose.

"Human for breakfast? Yuck," said Ant.

"Don't we have any honeysuckle?" asked Bee.

Ladybug shouted, "Air Group Leader! Dragonfly! Hurry! Uh, scramble! Do something!"

Dragonfly, instantly alert, dived to intercept Spider. He grabbed her and swung her, still attached to the strand of web, up to a limb of the oak.

He shook with anger. "How dare you? You ungrateful eight eyes! That human saved the Forest! And you're going to eat him?"

Spider spoke calmly, with a great show of hurt innocence. "Eat him? My dear Dragonfly, what kind of bloodthirsty arachnid do you think I am? I wanted to thank him."

"Does this mean there isn't any breakfast?" asked Ant.

"Hush, all of you," said Ladybug.

In the middle of the commotion, Ana awoke, and sat up, rubbing her eyes. "What a terrible dream I had," she said.

Zac blinked awake, and yawned. "I know. I think I had it too."

Surely, they thought, it had been a dream. Here they were, as usual, in their cozy home in the great oak, and at the foot of the bed, as usual, their beloved doth snoozed under the covers.

Ana pulled back the covers to wake Pook, anticipating his sloppy good morning kiss. But the lump at the foot of the bed wasn't Pook; it was just a pillow stuffed under the covers where Pook should have been. Then, the horrible memories came back, and so did the tears. It hadn't been a dream. Pook was gone, forever.

Zac sank back into the bed and stared up into Yorah's leaves. He could see his new friend, Ladybug. And someone accompanied her—another ladybug, slightly more brown in color. He pointed for Ana to see.

Ana thought—and Zac heard her thoughts—how sweet, a ladybug husband and wife.

Then, in through the window and up into the branches, flew a firefly and a beetle, carrying a caterpillar, a bee, carrying a snail . . . followed by a dragonfly with a spider on her back, a beetle, and finally a grasshopper riding on a glittering hummingbird. Zac and Ana watched them all rejoin their mates in Yorah's branches.

"The jewels!" Zac said, jumping out of bed. "They're alive!"

"What?" said Ana.

Now Yorah laughed, and shouted, "Take a look at me, sweeties! Look at these leaves of mine! They're green again. And they're growing. The rain washed away the blight! I feel so young—hardly a day over two hundred!"

In truth, the Great Forest, the trees, flowers and creatures were coming back to life.

Ana turned to Zac, a finger to her lips. "Listen! Birds!"

And soon they heard more—panting and flapping of wings. And then a thump.

Ana and Zac both wondered what could be thumping? Something clumsy tumbled down through Yorah's leaves. Then, as if catapulted from a limb, a furry white ball with wings shot through the window.

"Pook!"

The happy and very much alive little doth made a hard, three-bounce landing on the bed.

Pook, too, revived by the miraculous rain had flown all night—in the dark—to be back with Zac and Ana.

Ana, Zac and Pook tumbled and hugged in the bed. It felt like old times. Above them, Yorah's face appeared, and she smiled proudly. She could see them all clearly now. Then, Kootenstoopits appeared on the bedroom floor, laughing Pickensrooters began to empty the dresser drawers, and Flower Fairies, holding hands and singing formed a circle around the bed.

Then, just as he had done in the birch grove, Pook jumped into Zac's arms, licked his face and smiled broadly.

The End

It felt like old times.

Epilogue:
Another Beginning

So the story ends—happily, as a Fairy Tale should.

Ana and Zachariah lived on in their cozy home in the great oak tree. Every day, Zac still went out with Pook to look for wood; but now there was plenty nearby and he and Ana were never far apart. Zac filled his workshop with wood and he made lots of beautiful boxes and toys that he sold in the village. Ana still talked with Yorah and sang with the Fairies and picked up after the Pickensrooters and Kootenstoopits.

Pook was still fat, but he never again feared the dark, and he always protected Zac and Ana from tam-o'jacks, grubinmoles and cawcats.

Yorah grew older and wiser.

Ladybug, Dragonfly, Spider and the other Forest Creatures lived with their loved ones near the linden stump beside the birch grove.

Without their leader, the wicked Darklings never left the grotto again. The evil Rusful's irreparably broken body lay near the mouth of the grotto where the brave Pook had fought him and the Forest grew lush and the clear stream soon washed away his remains.

Zac and Ana could always hear each other's thoughts and dreams. And, now, Zac believed in Fairies.

Appendix

The Jewels

The following twelve beautiful and valuable jewels were selected by me from all over the world and they are yours to find and keep.

Like in the story, they are hidden in twelve separate locations. Yet, as I have said before, they are all easily accessible and they are not buried but they are truly hidden. Nothing should be disturbed in anyway for you to find them. You needn't dig or pry or move anything and you don't need any special tools or knowledge.

All you need to do to find one of the jewels described in the following pages by Master Gemologist Appraiser® Donald A. Palmieri, GG, ASA, is to decipher the clues in the story and go to the exact location and find your gold token. The gold token contains the information you need to get your jewel.

Good luck in your search!

The Snail

The Snail is set with one 2.6 mm round Cabochon turquoise and two fancy intense pink diamonds weighing .36 carat, mounted in platinum settings. The snail is handmade with die struck sections and is engraved with a textured shell. The total finished weight is 15.78 grams. The piece is stamped with French Hallmarks and the name "JEPOSE" along with a serial number 5395.

The Ladybug

The Ladybug is handmade with retractable hinged wings set with six round cabochon natural Burmese rubies and fifty-one round diamonds weighing a total of approximately 1.00 carat. The body is clad in red, black and white enamel and the total finished weight is 13.51 grams.

The Grasshopper

The Grasshopper is handmade in the late 1800's and set with eighty-six 1.2 to 2.8 mm round demantoid

garnets, and twenty-five old European cut diamonds weighing approximately one half carat, and it has one ruby eye. The total finished weight is 17.61 grams. The piece is believed to be of English origin and the demantoid from the Ural Mountains.

The Ant

The Ant is set with three spessartite garnets weighing a total of 15.09 carat. Further articulated by two hundred and four near colorless pavé set diamond legs and

channel-set diamond joints weighing a total of 4.01 carat. The total finished weight is 15.16 grams.

The Hummingbird

The Hummingbird's pear shape body is a South Sea pearl surrounded by one hundred and thirty-two colorless pavé set diamonds weighing 1.13 carat, one hundred and eighteen pavé set fancy black diamonds weighing  1.21 carat, thirty-four pavé set fancy vivid yellow diamonds weighing 1.05 carats, one hundred and ten pavé set emeralds weighing 4.82 carat, and thirty-seven rubies weighing 1.73 carats.

The Dragonfly

The Dragonfly is set with a body of nineteen oval and  round mixed cut blue sapphires weighing 9.87 carat, articulated with one hundred and ninety-eight bead set colorless diamonds weighing 3.24 carat, with wings finished in faint blue plique-a-jour enameling. The total finished weight is 34.68 grams.

The Beetle

The Beetle's movable body riser is set with one cush-ion cut 9.61 carats Tanzanite surmounted by twelve near colorless diamonds weighing 3.68 carat, con-cealed under retractable enameled wings, further articulated with bead and pavé set colorless diamonds weighing 8.16 carat, two vivid yellow diamonds weighing .06 carat, and two hundred and thirty-four black diamonds weighing 8.60 carat. The total finished weight is 107.48 grams.

The Butterfly

The Butterfly is set with one 1.11 carat pear shaped diamond head, with four wings pavé set contain-ing three hundred and thirty-two blue sapphires weighing 15.66 carat, three hundred and thirty-seven colorless diamonds weighing 4.81 carat. The body is further articulated with black enameling and the total finished weight is 62.57 grams.

The Firefly

The Firefly is set with a 1.44 carat oval natural alexandrite head, joined by a

5.91 carat oval natural burmese Ruby and two round fancy vivid yellow diamonds weighing .73 carat, further articulated with thirty-six colorless diamonds weighing .21 carat. The wings are black enameled. The total finished weight 22.97 is grams.

The Caterpillar

The Caterpillar has seven movable segments each containing one oval cabochon peridot, two round fancy

green diamonds, and two round amethysts. The segments are further articulated with plique-a-jour enameling. The total finished weight is 44.24 grams.

The Spider

The Spider is set with one 6.36 carats natural Kashmir blue sapphire joined by a 21.23 carat light yellow diamond forming the body and is further articulated by four hundred and four pavé and bead set diamonds weighing

12.73 carat. The total finished weight is 34.77 grams.

The Bee

The Bee's body is a pear shaped Tahitian black cultured pearl surrounded by one hundred and seventy-one pavé set near colorless diamonds weighing 1.51 carat, sixty-eight pavé set fancy vivid yellow diamonds weighing 1.48 carat, and forty-three pavé set fancy black diamonds weighing 1.55 carats. The pairs of movable wings are finished with light blue plique-a-jour enameling. The total finished weight is 21.88 grams.

The Tokens

Once you have deciphered the clues in the story and go to the location described, you will find a solid gold token. The token tells you the location of the real jeweled treasure.

A TREASURE'S TROVE

Appraiser's Note: August 2004

After reviewing and analyzing the crystal creatures that comprise the jewels being offered in the National Treasure Hunt of A Treasure's Trove, it is with great professional satisfaction that I am offering this commentary for the benefit of those treasure hunters and jewel connoisseurs.

Three of the jewels were acquired previously in Europe and the United States by the author of A Treasure's Trove.

The Grasshopper is a full-fledged 'grown up' antique with rare Demantoid Garnets and a sprinkling of diamonds. This brooch is a treasure in and of itself for jewelry collectors.

The Ladybug is a perfect example of beauty and grace, and in excellent condition - even her movable parts.

The Snail is a mid 20th century work of pure fun and folly. Before arriving in the forest, he crowned his antennae with two rare and collectible fancy intense pink diamonds to add to his perfectly executed French body. This piece, too, is in mint condition.

The remaining items in the Crystal Creature Collection are newly designed and created exclusively for A Treasure's Trove.

Having had the duty and privilege of periodically

dropping in to the workrooms to examine each jewel for craftsmanship, quality and value, was indeed a pleasure.

These items were designed by the author during the creation of A Treasure's Trove. When it came time to transform the forest creatures from page to precious treasure, models were made, metals were rolled, hammered, twisted, heated, drilled, textured and polished. Rare and precious gemstones including Kashmir Sapphires, Burmese Rubies, handfuls of large and small diamonds - Fancy Intense Pink, Fancy Vivid Yellow, Fancy Green and Fancy Black Diamonds, Alexandrite, Garnets, Amethyst and Tanzanite were summoned from all parts of the gem producing centers around the world. Thousands of gemstones were examined, analyzed and sorted, in order to select the finest qualities and precision sizes to produce this rare, one-of-a-kind collection.

To speak of the Old World master jewelers, like Fabergé, Lalique and others who pioneered many of the costly, time-consuming methods that have immortalized their works and have virtually vanished in this technical age of mass produced jewelry making, is to be refreshed by the spirit and birth of A Treasure's Trove's creatures. Thanks to the author and creator of these forest beings, old world craftsmanship had the opportunity to be reborn in the comfortable workrooms of the Danbury Connecticut joaillier extraordinaire, "Jewelry Designs".

Under the direction of Master Jeweler, Robert Underhill, the "Jewelry Design" model makers, designers, stone setters and enamellists borrowed the techniques of Fabergé and Lalique to fashion such pieces as those containing movable and mechanical parts, virtually bringing life to these crystallized creatures, and the delicately tinted, transparent plique-a-jour enameling replicating the wings of the dragonfly, bee and others.

By accepting this commission as independent arbiter of the quality and value of this collection, my only regret is that my family and I are disqualified from joining the many thousands of you who will actively pursue the quest to solve the puzzle and discover one of these exquisite treasures to call your own.

Good Luck To You All!

Donald A. Palmieri, GG, ASA
Master Gemologist Appraiser®
President - Gem Certification & Appraisal Lab
       Gemological Appraisal Association, Inc.
       New York, NY

A TREASURE'S TROVE
Treasure Hunt Contest of Skill
Official Rules

1.   HOW TO PARTICIPATE IN THIS PROMOTION (the "Treasure Hunt"): Obtain a copy of the book A Treasure's Trove by Michael Stadther (the "Book"). Contained within the Book are clues to twelve puzzles that, when solved, will direct you to the location of twelve (12) hidden tokens. Each token is hidden in a different location. The tokens can each be redeemed for a valuable jewel or amulet selected by Sponsor. The tokens will be located in public places within the continental United States. The first person to locate a token, using their intellect and skill, who satisfies the eligibility requirements and follows the redemption instructions set forth below, will, upon verification, receive the jewel or amulet signified by the token. The potential finder must submit the claim personally; submissions through agents or third parties are not valid. The Book was first available to the public on November 15, 2004. The Treasure Hunt will run until all tokens are found and finders verified, or until December 31, 2007 (the "End Date"), whichever is sooner.

2.   ELIGIBILITY: Open to legal residents of the 50 United States, including the District of Columbia, except residents of the states of CT, MD, ND and VT. Finders may be required to execute an affidavit swearing to compliance with these eligibility requirements. Employees of Sponsor, their immediate family and household members (related or not), and agents participating in the creation of this Treasure Hunt, are not eligible to enter.

3.   DETAILS: Solutions to each of the twelve puzzles in the Book have been recorded and are maintained in a secure location. Solutions will be revealed after the End Date, either on the web site or in a subsequent publication. You can learn more about the Book and the Treasure Hunt by going to the web site at www.atreasurestrove.com.

4.   PARTICIPANT CONDUCT: Sponsor reserves the right, in its sole discretion, to disqualify any Participant who (a) tampers with the entry process or the participation in, or operation of, the Treasure Hunt; (b) violates these rules; or (c) acts in a disruptive manner with the intent to annoy, abuse, threaten, or harass any other Participant or person. Tokens are located in public places, and are not in dangerous locations such as under water, on ledges, mountain tops or in caves. Destruction or destroying any real or personal property is not necessary in order to find the tokens or otherwise participate. Sponsor expressly forbids any such conduct. By participating, you agree to be bound by these Official Rules and the decisions of Sponsor, which shall be final in all respects on all aspects pertaining to the Treasure Hunt. Sponsor shall have complete discretion to interpret these Official Rules and any other aspect of the Treasure Hunt, and expressly reserves the right to refuse to award the prize to anyone who in Sponsor's discretion is in breach of these Official Rules or otherwise fails satisfactorily to establish their eligibility to win.

5.   REDEMPTION INSTRUCTIONS: If you find a token before the End Date, you must initiate redemption within 30 days of finding it. If Sponsor discovers a token missing from its hiding place for over 30 days, the token cannot be redeemed. Upon finding a token, within 30 days, follow the instructions on the back of the token. You may be asked to provide your solutions to the puzzles which led you to the location where you found the token, and execute an affidavit of eligibility and liability/publicity release (where legal). If your responses are verified as accurate, and it is determined that you used your intellect and skill in order to solve the Treasure Hunt, provided you are in all other respects eligible to receive a prize, you will be declared a finder. You will be asked to fax a photocopy of the token along with your name, address and all other contact information. You must also send in the token as directed. You should keep copies of all correspondence and copies of the token for your records. Additional verification requirements and redemption instructions may be required. Finders must return the affidavit of eligibility and liability/publicity release within twenty one (21) days of first attempted notification of verification. For finders who are younger than the age of majority, prize will be awarded in the finder's name to his/her parent or legal guardian, and affidavits and releases must be signed by the finder's parent or legal guardian. Finders must give Sponsor permission to publicize finder's name and hometown as a condition of receiving the prize, unless prohibited by law. Finders may also be required to use their names and submis-

sions in advertising and marketing materials in all media in perpetuity, and may be required to participate in publicity events, except where prohibited by law. Sponsor may not confirm verification of finders until after End Date, and will not transfer actual possession of the jewels until after the End Date. The jewels will be on display until the End Date, after which time verified finders may take possession of them.

6.   COLLABORATIONS: If you have collaborated in your efforts with other persons, each of the finding participants must comply with all of the foregoing requirements and execute all of the required documents. Collaborators must also release Sponsor from any liability in connection with their agreement among one another, and if Sponsor incurs any costs or expenses, including legal expenses, in connection with collaborators' agreement, all collaborators agree to reimburse Sponsor for any and all such costs and expenses jointly and severally.

7.   PRIZES: Twelve (12) jewels will be available in the Treasure Hunt.

Jewels	Appraised Retail Value	Cash Substitution value
Spider	$450,000	$135,000
Firefly	$280,000	$84,000
Beetle	$54,000	$16,200
Grasshopper	$50,000	$15,000
Butterfly	$46,000	$13,800
Dragonfly	$25,000	$7,500
Hummingbird	$23,000	$6,900
Bumble Bee	$22,300	$6,690
Ant	$19,900	$5,970
Caterpillar	$12,000	$4,000
Snail	$12,000	$4,000
Ladybug	$8,500	$2,550

Finders may elect to receive instead of the jewel the cash substitution value listed above. All federal, state and local taxes associated with the receipt or use of any prize and participation in the Treasure Hunt are the sole responsibility of the finder. IRS regulations require Sponsor to issue a 1099 tax form to anyone receiving any of the prizes available in this contest.

8.   GENERAL: All materials and submissions to Sponsor, including the tokens, become property of the Sponsor and will not be returned. Sponsor accepts no liability for submissions, correspondence or attempted redemptions that are late, lost, or otherwise misdirected, or not submitted in accordance with these Official Rules. If any tokens are not located by the End Date, or if no verified winner claims a token or a prize, Sponsor will donate the cash substitution to a charity of Sponsor's choice. No transfer or substitution of prizes permitted by winners, except as indicated herein. Sponsor has made extensive efforts and taken reasonable steps to ensure that the tokens remain where they are hidden until found by participants in this Contest. Sponsor will also, at various times during the promotion period, attempt to confirm that unclaimed tokens remain in their respective hidden locations. However, tokens may be moved by forces, including human intervention (intentional and unintentional) as well as force majeure events, over which Sponsor has no control. Sponsor disclaims all liability if, due to forces outside its control, a token is moved from its location. Sponsor may or may not, in its discretion, replace a token that has been moved but remains unclaimed with a new token.

9.   ADDITIONAL LIMITATIONS: By entering, participants (a) agree to be bound by the official rules and the decisions of the Sponsor which are final and binding in all respects; (b) agree to release Sponsor and agents from any and all liability, loss, damage or injury resulting from participation in this Treasure Hunt and searching for the tokens, as well as awarding, receipt, possession use and/or misuse of any prize awarded herein and acknowledge that Sponsor, and agents have neither made nor are in any manner responsible or liable for any warranty, representation, or guarantee, express or implied, in fact or in law, relative to any prize including, but not limited to, its quality, mechanical condition or fitness for a particular purpose; and (c) consent to use of his/her name, photograph and/or likeness for advertising and promotional purposes without additional com-

pensation, unless prohibited by law.

10.   DISPUTES. This Treasure Hunt is governed by the laws of the United States and the State of New York, without respect to conflict of law doctrines. As a condition of participating in this Treasure Hunt, participants agree that any and all disputes which cannot be resolved between the parties, and causes of action arising out of or in connection with this Treasure Hunt, shall be resolved individually, without resort to any form of class action, exclusively before a court located in New York County, New York having jurisdiction. Further, in any such dispute, under no circumstances will participants be permitted to obtain awards for, and hereby waive all rights to claim punitive, incidental or consequential damages, including attorneys' fees, other than participant's actual out-of-pocket expenses (e.g. costs associated with entering), and participant further waives all rights to have damages multiplied or increased.

11.   PUBLICATION OF FINDERS: After the End Date of the Treasure Hunt, the finders will be published on the web site.

12.   SPONSOR: The Sponsor of this Treasure Hunt is Treasure Trove, Inc., 3000 Marcus Avenue, Suite 1E5, Lake Success, NY 11042.